A FIGHT
WITH A CANNON

_____

by

VICTOR HUGO

British Library Cataloguing-in-Publication Data
A catalogue record for this book is available from
the British Library

Victor Hugo

Victor Marie Hugo was born on 26th February 1802, in Besançon, Franche-Comté, France. He was a political campaigner, artist, poet, novelist and dramatist of the Romantic movement, considered one of the greatest French writers of all time.

Hugo's father was a freethinking republican who considered Napoléon a hero, and his mother was a Catholic Royalist, who was executed in 1812 for plotting against the legendary general. Hugo's childhood was a period of national political turmoil. Napoléon was proclaimed Emperor two years after Hugo's birth, and the Bourbon Monarchy was restored before his eighteenth birthday. The opposing political and religious views of Hugo's parents reflected the forces that would battle for supremacy in France throughout his life.

As a young man, his mother dominated his education and upbringing, and as a result Hugo's early work in poetry and fiction reflects her passionate devotion to both King and Faith. It was only later, during the events leading up to France's 1848 Revolution, that he would begin to rebel against his Catholic Royalist education and instead champion Republicanism and Freethought. Hugo was also a rebellious young man, and on falling in love with his childhood friend Adèle Foucher (1803–

1868), became secretly engaged against his mothers wishes. Because of his close relationship with his mother, Hugo waited until after his mother's death (in 1821) to marry Adèle in 1822.

Hugo published his first novel the year following his marriage (*Han d'Islande*, 1823), and his second three years later (*Bug-Jargal*, 1826). Between 1829 and 1840 he would publish five more volumes of poetry, cementing his reputation as one of the greatest elegiac and lyric poets of his time. Victor Hugo's first mature work of fiction appeared in 1829, and reflected the acute social conscience that would infuse his later work. *The Last Day of a Condemned Man* would have a profound influence on later writers such as Albert Camus, Charles Dickens, and Fyodor Dostoevsky. It was soon followed by *The Hunchback of Notre-Dame* (in 1831), which was quickly translated into other language across Europe.

Adèle and Victor Hugo had their first child, Léopold, in 1823, but the boy died in infancy. The following year, on 28th August 1824, the couple's second child, Léopoldine was born, followed by Charles in 1826, François-Victor in 1828, and Adèle in 1830. Hugo's oldest and favourite daughter, Léopoldine, died at the age of nineteen in 1843, shortly after her marriage to Charles Vacquerie. On 4th September 1843, she drowned in the Seine at Villequier, pulled down by her heavy skirts, when a boat overturned. Her young husband also died trying to save her. The death left her father devastated; Hugo was travelling with his mistress at the time in the south of France, and first learned about Léopoldine's death from a newspaper he read in a cafe.

Hugo wrote many poems about his daughter's tragic life and death, and many biographers have claimed that he never completely recovered from this traumatic incident. His most famous poem is probably *Demain, Dès L'aube*, in which he describes visiting her grave. He began planning a major novel about social misery and injustice as early as the 1830s, but it would take a full seventeen years for *Les Misérables* to be realized and finally published in 1862. On its publication, the critical establishment was generally hostile to the novel, with Gustave Flaubert claiming he found within it 'neither truth nor greatness' and Baudelaire castigating it as 'tasteless and inept.' Despite this, *Les Misérables* was a massive hit with the public, and today remains Victor Hugo's most enduringly popular work.

After three unsuccessful attempts, Hugo was finally elected to the Académie Française in 1841, solidifying his position in the world of French arts and letters. He was also elevated to the peerage by King Louis-Philippe in the same year and entered the Higher Chamber as a *pair de France*, where he spoke against the death penalty and social injustice, and in favour of freedom of the press and self-government for Poland. In 1848, Hugo was elected to the Parliament as a conservative. In 1849 he broke with the conservatives when he gave a noted speech calling for the end of misery and poverty. When Louis Napoleon (Napoleon III) seized complete power in 1851, establishing an anti-parliamentary constitution, Hugo openly declared him a traitor to France.

Hugo decided to live in exile after Napoleon III's coup d'état at the end of 1851. After leaving France, he lived in Brussels briefly in 1851, before moving to the Channel Islands, first to Jersey (1852–1855) and then to the smaller island of Guernsey in 1855, where he stayed until 1870. Whilst in exile, Hugo published his famous political pamphlets against Napoleon

III, *Napoléon le Petit* and *Histoire d'un Crime,* which whilst banned in France, had a strong impact. Although Napoleon III proclaimed a general amnesty in 1859, the author stayed in exile, only returning when Napoleon was forced from power in 1870. Hugo's next novel, *Troilers of the Sea* turned away from the social and political themes so prevalent in *Les Miserables.* It told the story of a man hoping to gain the approval of his beloved's father by rescuing his ship - thus battling the elements, mythical beasts and the sea itself. It was published in 1866, and was dedicated to the channel islands, in which Hugo found such a welcoming home.

Hugo returned to political and social issues in his next novel, *The Man Who Laughs*, which was published in 1869 and painted a critical picture of the aristocracy. The novel was not as successful as his previous efforts, and Hugo himself began to comment on the growing distance between himself and literary contemporaries such as Flaubert and Émile Zola, whose realist and naturalist novels were now exceeding the popularity of his own work. After the Siege of Paris, Hugo lived again in Guernsey from 1872 to 1873, before finally returning to France for the remainder of his life. His last novel, *Ninety-Three*, published in 1874, dealt with a subject that Hugo had previously avoided: the Reign of Terror during the French Revolution. Though Hugo's popularity was on the decline at the time of its publication, many now consider *Ninety-Three* to be a work on par with his earlier and better-known novels.

When Hugo returned to Paris in 1870, the country hailed him as a national hero. This was a sad time for the ageing writer however, as within a brief period he suffered a mild stoke, his daughter Adèle's internment in an insane asylum, and the death of his two sons. His wife Adèle had died in 1868. Hugo's mistress, Juliette Drouet, also died in 1883 – two years before Hugo's own death. Despite this, to honour the fact that he was entering his eightieth year, in 1882, one of the greatest tributes to a living writer was held. The celebrations began on 25th June when Hugo was presented with a Sèvres vase, the traditional gift for sovereigns, and on 27th June one of the largest parades in French history was held.

Victor Hugo's death from pneumonia on 22nd May 1885, at the age of eighty-three, generated intense national mourning. He was not only revered as a towering figure in literature, but he was also a statesman who shaped the Third Republic and democracy in France. More than two million people joined his funeral procession in Paris from the Arc de Triomphe to the Panthéon, where he was buried. He shares a crypt within the with Alexandre Dumas and Émile Zola.

A FIGHT WITH A CANNON

La vieuville was suddenly cut short by a cry of despair, and a the same time a noise was heard wholly unlike any other sound. The cry and sounds came from within the vessel.

The captain and lieutenant rushed toward the gun-deck but could not get down. All the gunners were pouring up in dismay.

Something terrible had just happened.

One of the carronades of the battery, a twenty-four pounder, had broken loose.

This is the most dangerous accident that can possibly take place on shipboard. Nothing more terrible can happen to a sloop of was in open sea and under full sail.

A cannon that breaks its moorings suddenly becomes some strange, supernatural beast. It is a machine transformed into a monster. That short mass on wheels moves like a billiard-ball, rolls with the rolling of the ship, plunges with the pitching goes, comes, stops, seems to meditate, starts on its course again, shoots like an arrow from one end of the vessel to the other, whirls around, slips away, dodges, rears, bangs, crashes, kills, exterminates. It is a battering ram capriciously assaulting a wall. Add to this the fact that the ram is of metal, the wall of wood.

It is matter set free; one might say, this eternal slave was avenging itself; it seems as if the total depravity concealed in what we call inanimate things has escaped, and burst forth all of a sudden; it appears to lose patience, and to take a strange mysterious revenge; nothing more relentless than this wrath of the inanimate. This enraged lump leaps like a panther, it has the clumsiness of an elephant, the nimbleness of a mouse, the obstinacy of an ox, the uncertainty of the billows, the zigzag of the lightning, the deafness of the grave. It weighs ten thousand pounds, and it rebounds like a child's ball. It spins and then abruptly darts off at right angles.

And what is to be done? How put an end to it? A tempest ceases, a cyclone passes over, a wind dies down, a broken mast can be replaced, a leak can be stopped, a fire extinguished, but what will become of this enormous brute of bronze. How can it be captured? You can reason with a bulldog, astonish a bull, fascinate a boa, frighten a tiger, tame a lion; but you have no resource against this monster, a loose cannon. You can not kill it, it is dead; and at the same time it lives. It lives with a sinister life which comes to it from the infinite. The deck beneath it gives it full swing. It is moved by the ship, which is moved by the sea, which is moved by the wind. This destroyer is a toy. The ship, the waves, the winds, all play with it, hence its frightful animation. What is to be done with this apparatus? How fetter this stupendous engine of destruction? How anticipate its comings and goings, its returns, its stops, its shocks? Any one of its blows on the side of the ship may stave it in. How foretell its frightful meanderings? It is dealing with a projectile, which alters its mind, which seems to have ideas, and changes its direction every instant. How check the course of what must be avoided? The horrible cannon struggles, advances, backs, strikes right, strikes left, retreats, passes by, disconcerts expectation, grinds up obstacles, crushes men like flies. All the terror of the situation is in the fluctuations of the flooring. How fight an inclined plane subject to caprices? The ship has, so to speak, in its belly, an imprisoned thunderstorm, striving to escape; something like a thunderbolt rumbling above an earthquake.

In an instant the whole crew was on foot. It was the fault of the gun captain, who had neglected to fasten the screw-nut of the mooring-chain, and had insecurely clogged the four wheels of the gun carriage; this gave play to the sole and the framework, separated the two platforms, and the breeching. The tackle had given way, so that the cannon was no longer firm on its carriage. The stationary breeching, which prevents recoil, was not in use at this time. A heavy sea struck the port, the carronade, insecurely fastened, had recoiled and broken its chain, and began its terrible course over the deck.

To form an idea of this strange sliding, let one imagine a drop of water running over a glass.

At the moment when the fastenings gave way, the gunners were in the battery, some in groups, others scattered about, busied with the customary work among sailors getting ready for a signal for action. The carronade, hurled forward by the pitching of the vessel, made a gap in this crowd of men and crushed four at the first blow; then sliding back and shot out again as the ship rolled, it cut in two a fifth unfortunate, and knocked a piece of the battery against the larboard side with such force as to unship it. This caused the cry of distress just heard. All the men rushed to the companion-way. The gun-deck was vacated in a twinkling.

The enormous gun was left alone. It was given up to itself. It was its own master and master of the ship. It could do what it pleased. This whole crew, accustomed to laugh in time of battle, now trembled. To describe the terror is impossible.

Captain Boisberthelot and Lieutenant la Vieuville, although both dauntless men, stopped at the head of the companion-way and, dumb, pale, and hesitating, looked down on the deck below. Some one elbowed past and went down.

It was their passenger, the peasant, the man of whom they had just been speaking a moment before.

Reaching the foot of the companion-way, he stopped.

The cannon was rushing back and forth on the deck. One might have supposed it to be the living chariot of the Apocalypse. The marine lantern swinging overhead added a dizzy shifting of light and shade to the picture. The form of the cannon disappeared in the violence of its course, and it looked now black in the light, now mysteriously white in the darkness.

It went on in its destructive work. It had already shattered four other guns and made two gaps in the side of the ship, fortunately above the water-line, but where the water would come in, in case of heavy weather. It rushed frantically against the framework; the strong timbers withstood the shock; the curved shape of the wood gave them great power of resistance; but they creaked beneath the blows of this huge club, beating on all sides at once, with a strange sort of ubiquity. The percussions of a grain of shot shaken in a bottle are not swifter or more senseless. The four wheels passed back and forth over the dead men, cutting them, carving them, slashing them, till the five corpses were a score of stumps rolling across the deck; the heads of the dead men seemed to cry out; streams of blood curled over the deck with the rolling of the vessel; the planks, damaged in several places, began to gape open. The whole ship was filled with the horrid noise and confusion.

The captain promptly recovered his presence of mind and ordered everything that could check and impede the cannon's mad course to be thrown through the hatchway down on the gun-deck—mattresses, hammocks, spare sails, rolls of cordage, bags belonging to the crew, and bales of counterfeit assignats, of which the corvette carried a large quantity—a characteristic piece of English villany regarded as legitimate warfare.

But what could these rags do? As nobody dared to go below to dispose of them properly, they were reduced to lint in a few minutes.

There was just sea enough to make the accident as bad as possible. A tempest would have been desirable, for it might have upset the cannon, and with its four wheels once in the air there would be some hope of getting it under control. Meanwhile, the havoc increased.

There were splits and fractures in the masts, which are set into the framework of the keel and rise above the decks of ships like great, round pillars. The convulsive blows of the cannon had cracked the mizzenmast, and had cut into the mainmast.

The battery was being ruined. Ten pieces out of thirty were disabled; the breaches in the side of the vessel were increasing, and the corvette was beginning to leak.

The old passenger having gone down to the gun-deck, stood like a man of stone at the foot of the steps. He cast a stern glance over this scene of devastation. He did not move. It seemed impossible to take a step forward. Every movement of the loose carronade threatened the ship's destruction. A few moments more and shipwreck would be inevitable.

They must perish or put a speedy end to the disaster; some

course must be decided on; but what? What an opponent was this carronade! Something must be done to stop this terrible madness—to capture this lightning—to overthrow this thunderbolt.

Boisberthelot said to La Vieuville:

"Do you believe in God, chevalier?"

La Vieuville replied:

"Yes—no. Sometimes."

"During a tempest?"

"Yes, and in moments like this."

"God alone can save us from this," said Boisberthelot.

Everybody was silent, letting the carronade continue its horrible din.

Outside, the waves beating against the ship responded with their blows to the shocks of the cannon. It was like two hammers alternating.

Suddenly, in the midst of this inaccessible ring, where the escaped cannon was leaping, a man was seen to appear, with an iron bar in his hand. He was the author of the catastrophe, the captain of the gun, guilty of criminal carelessness, and the cause of the accident, the master of the carronade. Having done the mischief, he was anxious to repair it. He had seized the iron bar in one hand, a tiller-rope with a slip-noose in the other, and jumped, down the hatchway to the gun-deck.

Then began an awful sight; a Titanic scene; the contest between gun and gunner; the battle of matter and intelligence; the duel between man and the inanimate.

The man stationed himself in a corner, and, with bar and rope in his two hands, he leaned against one of the riders, braced himself on his legs, which seemed two steel posts; and livid, calm, tragic, as if rooted to the deck, he waited.

He waited for the cannon to pass by him.

The gunner knew his gun, and it seemed to him as if the gun ought to know him. He had lived long with it. How many times he had thrust his hand into its mouth! It was his own familiar monster. He began to speak to it as if it were his dog.

"Come!" he said. Perhaps he loved it.

He seemed to wish it to come to him.

But to come to him was to come upon him. And then he would be lost. How could he avoid being crushed? That was the question. All looked on in terror.

Not a breast breathed freely, unless perhaps that of the old man, who was alone in the battery with the two contestants, a stern witness.

He might be crushed himself by the cannon. He did not stir.

Beneath them the sea blindly directed the contest.

At the moment when the gunner, accepting this frightful hand-to-hand conflict, challenged the cannon, some chance rocking of the sea caused the carronade to remain for an instant motionless and as if stupefied. "Come, now!" said the man.

It seemed to listen.

Suddenly it leaped toward him. The man dodged the blow.

The battle began. Battle unprecedented. Frailty struggling against the invulnerable. The gladiator of flesh attacking the beast of brass. On one side, brute force; on the other, a human soul.

All this was taking place in semi-darkness. It was like the shadowy vision of a miracle.

A soul—strange to say, one would have thought the cannon

also had a soul; but a soul full of hatred and rage. This sightless thing seemed to have eyes. The monster appeared to lie in wait for the man. One would have at least believed that there was craft in this mass. It also chose its time. It was a strange, gigantic insect of metal, having or seeming to have the will of a demon. For a moment this colossal locust would beat against the low ceiling overhead, then it would come down on its four wheels like a tiger on its four paws, and begin to run at the man. He, supple, nimble, expert, writhed away like an adder from all these lightning movements. He avoided a collision, but the blows which he parried fell against the, vessel, and continued their work of destruction.

An end of broken chain was left hanging to the carronade. This chain had in some strange way become twisted about the screw of the cascabel. One end of the chain was fastened to the gun-carriage. The other, left loose, whirled desperately about the cannon, making all its blows more dangerous.

The screw held it in a firm grip, adding a thong to a battering-ram, making a terrible whirlwind around the cannon, an iron lash in a brazen hand. This chain complicated the contest.

However, the man went on fighting. Occasionally, it was the man who attacked the cannon; he would creep along the side of the vessel, bar and rope in hand; and the cannon, as if it understood, and as though suspecting some snare, would flee away. The man, bent on victory, pursued it.

Such things can not long continue. The cannon seemed to say to itself, all of a sudden, "Come, now! Make an end of it!" and it stopped. One felt that the crisis was at hand. The cannon, as if in suspense, seemed to have, or really had—for to all it was a living being—a ferocious malice prepense. It made a sudden, quick dash at the gunner. The gunner sprang out of the way, let it pass by, and cried out to it with a laugh, "Try it again!" The cannon, as if enraged, smashed a carronade on the port side; then, again seized by the invisible sling which controlled it, it was hurled to the starboard side at the man, who made his escape. Three carronades gave way under the blows of the cannon; then, as if blind and not knowing what more to do, it turned its back on the man, rolled from stern to bow, injured the stern and made a breach in the planking of the prow. The man took refuge at the foot of the steps, not far from the old man who was looking on. The gunner held his iron bar in rest. The cannon seemed to notice it, and without taking the trouble to turn around, slid back on the man, swift as the blow of an axe. The man, driven against the side of the ship, was lost. The whole crew cried out with horror.

But the old passenger, till this moment motionless, darted forth more quickly than any of this wildly swift rapidity. He seized a package of counterfeit assignats, and, at the risk of being crushed, succeeded in throwing it between the wheels of the carronade. This decisive and perilous movement could not have been made with more exactness and precision by a man trained in all the exercises described in Durosel's "Manual of Gun Practice at Sea."

The package had the effect of a clog. A pebble may stop a log, the branch of a tree turn aside an avalanche. The carronade stumbled. The gunner, taking advantage of this critical opportunity, plunged his iron bar between the spokes of one of the hind wheels. The cannon stopped. It leaned forward. The man, using the bar as a lever, held it in equilibrium. The heavy mass was overthrown, with the crash of a falling bell, and the man, rushing with all his might, dripping with perspiration, passed the slipnoose around the bronze neck of the subdued monster.

It was ended. The man had conquered. The ant had control over the mastodon; the pygmy had taken the thunderbolt prisoner.

The mariners and sailors clapped their hands.

The whole crew rushed forward with cables and chains, and in an instant the cannon was secured.

The gunner saluted the passenger.

"Sir," he said, "you have saved my life."

The old man had resumed his impassive attitude, and made no reply.

The man had conquered, but the cannon might be said to have conquered as well. Immediate shipwreck had been avoided, but the corvette was not saved. The damage to the vessel seemed beyond repair. There were five breaches in her sides, one, very large, in the bow; twenty of the thirty carronades lay useless in their frames. The one which had just been captured and chained again was disabled; the screw of the cascabel was sprung, and consequently leveling the gun made impossible. The battery was reduced to nine pieces. The ship was leaking. It was necessary to repair the damages at once, and to work the pumps.

The gun-deck, now that one could look over it, was frightful to behold. The inside of an infuriated elephant's cage would not be more completely demolished.

However great might be the necessity of escaping observation, the necessity of immediate safety was still more imperative to the corvette. They had been obliged to light up the deck with lanterns hung here and there on the sides.

However, all the while this tragic play was going on, the crew were absorbed by a question of life and death, and they were wholly ignorant of what was taking place outside the vessel. The fog had grown thicker; the weather had changed; the wind had worked its pleasure with the ship; they were out of their course, with Jersey and Guernsey close at hand, further to the south than they ought to have been, and in the midst of a heavy sea. Great billows kissed the gaping wounds of the vessel—kisses full of danger. The rocking of the sea threatened destruction. The breeze had become a gale. A squall, a tempest, perhaps, was brewing. It was impossible to see four waves ahead.

While the crew were hastily repairing the damages to the gun-deck, stopping the leaks, and putting in place the guns which had been uninjured in the disaster, the old passenger had gone on deck again.

He stood with his back against the mainmast.

He had not noticed a proceeding which had taken place on the vessel. The Chevalier de la Vieuville had drawn up the marines in line on both sides of the mainmast, and at the sound of the boatswain's whistle the sailors formed in line, standing on the yards.

The Count de Boisberthelot approached the passenger.

Behind the captain walked a man, haggard, out of breath, his dress disordered, but still with a look of satisfaction on his face.

It was the gunner who had just shown himself so skilful in subduing monsters, and who had gained the mastery over the cannon.

The count gave the military salute to the old man in peasant's dress, and said to him:

"General, there is the man."

The gunner remained standing, with downcast eyes, in military attitude.

The Count de Boisberthelot continued:

"General, in consideration of what this man has done, do you not think there is something due him from his commander?"

"I think so," said the old man.

"Please give your orders," replied Boisberthelot.

"It is for you to give them, you are the captain."

"But you are the general," replied Boisberthelot.

The old man looked at the gunner.

"Come forward," he said.

The gunner approached.

The old man turned toward the Count de Boisberthelot, took off the cross of Saint-Louis from the captain's coat and fastened it on the gunner's jacket.

"Hurrah!" cried the sailors.

The mariners presented arms.

And the old passenger, pointing to the dazzled gunner, added:

"Now, have this man shot."

Dismay succeeded the cheering.

Then in the midst of the death-like stillness, the old man raised his voice and said:

"Carelessness has compromised this vessel. At this very hour it is perhaps lost. To be at sea is to be in front of the enemy. A ship making a voyage is an army waging war. The tempest is concealed, but it is at hand. The whole sea is an ambuscade. Death is the penalty of any misdemeanor committed in the face of the enemy. No fault is reparable. Courage should be rewarded, and negligence punished."

These words fell one after another, slowly, solemnly, in a sort of inexorable metre, like the blows of an axe upon an oak.

And the man, looking at the soldiers, added:

"Let it be done."

The man on whose jacket hung the shining cross of Saint-Louis bowed his head.

At a signal from Count de Boisberthelot, two sailors went below and came back bringing the hammock-shroud; the chaplain, who since they sailed had been at prayer in the officers' quarters, accompanied the two sailors; a sergeant detached twelve marines from the line and arranged them in two files, six by six; the gunner, without uttering a word, placed himself between the two files. The chaplain, crucifix in hand, advanced and stood beside him. "March," said the sergeant. The platoon marched with slow steps to the bow of the vessel. The two sailors, carrying the shroud, followed. A gloomy silence fell over the vessel. A hurricane howled in the distance.

A few moments later, a light flashed, a report sounded through the darkness, then all was still, and the sound of a body falling into the sea was heard.

The old passenger, still leaning against the mainmast, had crossed his arms, and was buried in thought.

Boisberthelot pointed to him with the forefinger of his left hand, and said to La Vieuville in a low voice:

"La Vendée has a head."